"Don't you wish you had a candy bar right now?" I asked.

"Yes, but . . ."

"Open your hand," I demanded, grabbing her arm.

She obeyed.

"Nothing in it, right?" I asked.

I closed my eyes and wished for a chocolate bar.

Before I opened them, I heard her cry out.

"Wow!" Janie exclaimed. "How'd you do that?" She tore open the wrapper and took a bite.

Then looked up at me. "We've got to talk," she said.

# WISH
# MAGIC

# WISH MAGIC

by Elizabeth Koehler-Pentacoff
illustrated by R. W. Alley

**little rainbow**®
Troll

For Mom and Dad
—E. K. P.

# Chapter
# 1

"Don't blow up the house, Morris," said Mom. "It's not paid for yet."

Morris blinked behind the frames of his thick glasses. He was reading a book called *All About Combustion*. "I'll try not to," he said.

"Come *on*, Morris," I said. We were late again, as usual.

Morris grabbed his things from the table. I ran out the door without even a bit of breakfast.

"Hey, Meg," cried Morris, running behind me.

The bus pulled up just as we reached the curb.

"What?" I puffed.

Morris shoved a sugar doughnut in my face. "Here. Have some breakfast."

I paused at the open door of the bus. Since when did my geeky brother ever think of me? I looked at the doughnut suspiciously. Was this a trick?

"Mom got them for us at the bakery," he said. "I already had mine."

My stomach growled. "Thanks," I said, reaching for it with my free hand.

The bus was crowded, but my best friend Janie had saved me a seat. I finished the doughnut and licked my fingers clean.

"Did you finish your book report?" Janie asked.

"Oh, no!" I said, groaning. "I forgot all about it." The doughnut I had eaten felt like lead in my stomach.

I worried about it all morning. Stupid me. I had read the book, too.

Morris was so smart, he always got straight A's. If only I could remember to do the work, I would get good grades, too.

After lunch Mrs. Halstead told us to hand the book reports in.

Maybe I should just pretend I lost it. I could shuffle papers around in my desk. I could make an excuse of some kind. I was good at that.

I opened my desk, pretending to look for the report.

"Pass your reports forward, please," said Mrs. Halstead.

Feeling sick, I closed my eyes and wished I'd completed it.

When I opened them, the report was right in front of me.

In my own handwriting.

My name, Meg Schuster, was in the corner, with today's date written below it.

"My book report is on *The Island of the Blue Dolphins*," I read silently. My eyes skimmed down the page. A summary followed a personal opinion of the book. And there were no spelling mistakes. None that I could see, that is.

"Pass your papers in, please," called Mrs. Halstead from the front of the room.

I swallowed nervously. How could this be? I handed the paper forward to Dwayne, who sat in front of me. He turned around and made a gruesome face by touching the tip of his nose with his tongue. Then he faced Mrs. Halstead, looking innocent as always. He was the boy with a thousand faces. That kid never got caught. Never.

The bell rang and I followed everyone out to the lockers.

"Meg, Meg!" shouted Janie. She popped a piece of grape bubblegum in her mouth. "Want to go to the skating rink?"

I pushed the book report from my mind and focused on Janie. "Gee, I can't," I said. "I left my skates at home."

"Drat," she said, opening our locker door and blowing a bubble.

"I wish my skates were here," I said absentmindedly.

"What do you mean?" Janie asked.

I followed her stare to the bottom of our locker. There were my ice skates right on top of my spelling book.

I clutched her arm. "But Janie . . . I . . . I . . . I really left them at home."

"Well, then what are they doing here?" She laughed and handed me my skates. "Did they skate over here by themselves? Come on, let's go."

"First I have to call my mom and ask if it's O.K.," I said, searching for change in my purse.

What's going on, I wondered. I know I didn't carry those skates to school today. I could even picture them on the rug right by the front door of my house.

"Oh, great," I said aloud.

Janie put her jacket on and closed the locker. "What's wrong?"

"I don't have change for a phone call."

Janie felt her pants pocket. "Me neither. I used my money for a candy bar."

"I wish I had a quarter," I said.

And then I felt it in my hand. I knew it was a quarter without even looking at it.

Lifting my hand, I saw a shiny new twenty-five cent piece. Locker doors slammed and "byes" echoed down the hallway.

Janie glanced down at my open palm. "Oh, good. You found one." She headed for the pay phone near the bathrooms.

"No, I wished for it," I whispered, gazing at the quarter.

Janie reached the phone. "What's the matter? Come on!" She cracked her gum.

"In a minute." I wanted to try something first.

Quickly, I closed my eyes and wished for another quarter. I opened my clenched hand and saw two quarters.

I gasped. Wish magic. I wished . . . and it happened.

"Hey Meg, are you all right?" Janie had a puzzled expression on her face as she walked toward me. "Are you going to call your mom?"

"Yeah sure," I replied. I slid the other quarter into my purse. Maybe I'd better figure out what was happening before I told anyone. After all, there could be a good explanation. Maybe it was like one of those movies where the picture gets all wavy and suddenly the star snaps out of a dream.

Or maybe I was going crazy.

# Chapter 2

When we reached the rink, I had the perfect chance to test the magic again. Although I really like to skate, I fall a lot. I had plenty of bumps and black and blue marks all over my legs and bottom to prove it, too. But Janie flew on the ice. She knew how to do a split jump and a double toe loop by the time she was nine. I was still learning how to skate backwards.

After I laced my skates, Janie whizzed off. I wobbled onto the ice and gripped the side rail. My weak ankles touched the ice. Closing my eyes, I wished. I felt my muscles tighten. Cautiously peeking through my closed lids, I glanced at my feet. My ankles were actually straight and strong!

I let got of the hand rail and began to skate. It felt as though my feet had a mind of their own. Left, right, left, right, I glided across the ice, easily passing Janie. Her mouth dropped open and she came to a stop. Other skaters turned to watch me.

Suddenly, I was the only one skating. Round and round I flew. And then I slowed to do a triple axle. Janie gasped. As I twirled in front of her, faster and faster, spinning nearly out of control, I closed my eyes and wished not to crash.

I didn't. I came to a graceful stop, hands curved up above me in a skaters' pose. The audience clapped.

Blushing, I dropped my arms, and quickly skated to Janie.

"Wow. What happened to you?" she cried. "Did you take private lessons? Why didn't you tell me about it? When did this happen?" Her sentences rushed out, piling on top of each other.

"I'll tell you later," I said under my breath, noticing a crowd had gathered around us.

We changed into our shoes and headed out the door.

"I can't stand it any longer," Janie said, her voice raising an octave. "What's the big secret? Where did you learn to skate like that?"

I shrugged. "Just practice, I guess."

On the sidewalk outside, I looked around. No one was near. Janie combed her fingers through her brown hair.

"I don't get it," Janie persisted. "How come you've been bad for so long and now all of a sudden . . ." Her voice trailed off.

"Bad?" I asked. "Gee, thanks a lot." I set my skates down on the grass and bent to tie my tennis shoe.

My best friend cleared her throat. "Not exactly BAD, but not very good either."

"That's true," I admitted.

"So what did you do?"

"I'll tell you, but you have to cross your heart and hope to die that you'll never ever tell anyone."

Janie raised her eyebrows and laughed. "Sure. But why the big secret? Is it magic or something?"

I was quiet for a moment. "Yes," I finally said. "At least I think so."

"Magic? Right. Like *Bewitched* on TV." Janie chuckled and shifted her books in her arm. "How come I didn't see you twitch your nose?"

"Not exactly that kind of magic."

"Oh, come on, Meg, stop fooling around," Janie said. "Who's your new teacher?"

I lifted my skates and waited for a couple of kids to pass by. "It's magic, Janie. And I can prove it."

"Why don't you turn yourself into a bird and fly away?" she scoffed, as we continued down the sidewalk.

I felt hurt. My best friend didn't believe me! I kicked a stone on the sidewalk. Suddenly, Janie began to get irritating. I was sick of the sound of gum snapping as she talked.

I stopped walking and turned to her. "Don't you ever get tired of that horrible smelling bubblegum?"

"Huh?" said Janie, surprised.

"I'll get rid of it for you." I closed my eyes and wished.

Janie gasped. She grabbed her throat. "Did I

swallow it? My gum is gone! Where did it go?"

"Well, I don't know about you, but I'm hungry," I said. I was in the mood to show off, now that I had her attention. Maybe she'd really believe me if I whipped up something fun.

A puzzled frown appeared on Janie's face.

"Don't you wish you had a candy bar right now?" I asked.

"Yes, but . . ."

"Open your hand," I demanded, grabbing her arm.

She obeyed.

"Nothing in it, right?" I asked.

I closed my eyes and wished for a chocolate bar.

Before I opened them, I heard her cry out.

"Wow!" Janie exclaimed. "How'd you do that?" She tore open the wrapper and took a bite.

Then she looked up at me. "We've got to talk," she said.

# Chapter 3

The minute I shut my bedroom door, Janie started asking questions.

"When did this start? How come you're magic all of a sudden? Does anyone else know? What are you going to do now?"

I flopped on my bed and stared at the ceiling. "This afternoon, I don't know, no, and I have no idea."

Janie blinked. "What?"

"Everything started this afternoon. I don't know why or how, and no one knows about this but you." Frowning, I shook my finger at her. "And remember, you promised not to tell anyone."

Janie isn't very good at keeping secrets. Last year she bought me a T-shirt for my birthday. She dropped hints for two days, then told me three weeks before my party.

"Don't worry," she said, crossing her legs next to me. "This will stay between you and me. Just think—you can do anything now!"

"I don't know about that. What if it doesn't last?" I traced the pattern on my quilt with my fingers.

"Then start wishing fast. You could wish for a million dollars . . ."

Sitting up, I said, "But, Janie, people would get suspicious if I suddenly had all this money. Where would I say it came from?"

Janie chewed her gum, deep in thought. "A rich uncle?"

"No, Janie. My mom would know the truth. I have to keep it to small wishes."

Her eyes sparkled. "Make a wish now."

# Chapter
# 4

"Eeech, eeech," the animal screeched, swinging from branch to branch on a palm tree. A giggle rose in my throat.

"I've never seen a purple polka-dotted monkey before," Janie said as she threw her head back and laughed.

My mother's voice filtered up the stairway. "Megan! Megan!"

"Eeech, eeech," the monkey cried.

"Shh!" I told him. "My mother's coming." Beneath the screeches I could hear the creaks of the stairs.

"Quick," advised Janie. "Wish him away."

I closed my eyes and wished. When I opened them, the monkey and palm tree were gone.

My mother knocked on the door. "Meg, are you all right?" She stuck her head in the room.

Janie said, "Hi, Mrs. Schuster."

"Hi, Janie." She turned to me. "What were those strange sounds I heard up here?"

"Sounds?" I said. "What sounds?"

Janie said, "Oh, the screeching? We're practicing our skit about wild animals for class."

Mom smiled. "That sounds like fun. Well, when you're through practicing, you can come down for a snack."

"Thanks, Mom," I said.

After she left, we flopped down on the bed.

Janie unwrapped a new piece of grape bubblegum and popped it into her mouth. "Want one?"

"No, thanks." I wound a strand of hair around my index finger. "You know, we're going to have to be more careful with this magic business."

"Yeah." Janie blew a bubble. "We almost got caught."

"And you know parents. If it's fun, they'd want to take it away."

"Or your mom would call doctors to examine you."

I chuckled. "And then they'd put me in some laboratory and study me like they do rats."

"So what are you going to do next?"

I heard a buzzing noise from the next room.

"What's that?" asked Janie.

"The stupid computer in Morris's room. He loves to work on his experiments all day long. And sometimes in the middle of the night."

"Your brother sure is a brain."

Next we heard a mechanical voice. I sighed. "That computer talks to him all the time. It drives me crazy! It's even worse than Morris."

Janie put her ear to the wall. Her eyes widened. "You know what? Morris talks back to it."

"Tell me about it. They talk science together. But that's not as bad as when Morris shows off in front of other people."

Janie shook her head sympathetically. "How awful."

"I get so sick of his bragging." I leaned straight up against the wall. "And I can't understand half of what he says."

The buzzing and mechanical voice in the other room stopped. Then everything was quiet. Too quiet.

# *Chapter*
# 5

Janie frowned. "What's the matter?"

I pointed to my bedroom door and said loudly, "What's our math assignment?"

I placed my hand on the doorknob and swung the door open with a jerk.

Morris fell into the room. Janie gasped.

"Why don't you mind your own business, Mr. Snoopynose?" I yelled.

He grabbed his pen and notebook and ran down the stairs.

I shook my head. "Morris gets more strange every day."

* * *

At school the next morning, I took out my long division problems. I had done them by wish magic.

"Psst."

Turning, I saw Janie mouth the word 'help' and she held up her partially finished assignment.

I nodded, closed my eyes, and wished. Janie examined the paper and smiled.

"Thanks," she whispered.

I flashed the OK sign just before Mrs. Halstead collected the homework.

Dwayne swiveled in his seat. He pulled his bottom eyelids down with his fingers and stuck out his tongue.

Yuck! What he'd do for attention.

I wished quickly. It worked.

"Dwayne Ferguson," called Mrs. Halstead.

Dwayne dropped his hands to his desk.

"Come up here," she ordered.

The class tittered.

Dwayne rose from his seat and sauntered to Mrs. Halstead. "Since you love making faces so much, you can make them right here."

"What?" asked Dwayne.

"Stand here." Mrs. Halstead took his

shoulders in her hands and positioned Dwayne in front of the room. "Now, while we're copying the spelling words from the board, you may entertain us with the same expression you created for Meg."

For a moment he just stood still. The class didn't utter a sound. Mrs. Halstead had never given punishment like this before.

"Go on," said Mrs. Halstead.

So Dwayne recreated the monster. Mrs. Halstead grinned. Seeing her grinning like that with Dwayne looking so stupid, it made us all crack up. Dwayne's monster face turned red, but he held his position.

"Class, write the words and sentences from the blackboard onto your paper. Tomorrow we'll have the pre–test."

As we copied the words, occasionally someone would giggle in the room. Mrs. Halstead didn't say anything. She just sat at her desk correcting papers.

When the bell rang, we all filed past Dwayne, frozen in his position. The snickering turned to a wild roar once we hit the hallway.

Janie whooped. "Did you ever see anything so funny?"

"Mrs. Halstead was great today, wasn't she?" said Madeline.

Mike closed his locker with a bang. "Boy, I'd give anything for a picture of Dwayne with that stupid look on his face."

Janie's eyes danced with excitement. I closed mine briefly and then opened my notebook. There, among my spelling words, was a color photograph of Dwayne.

"Here." I handed the picture to Mike.

Looking down, he whistled. "Wow. That's great! Hey, I didn't see you take that picture. When did you do it?"

Members of the class crowded around us, studying the picture.

"So where's your camera?" Madeline asked me.

"In my desk," I answered, wishing before I spoke so it wouldn't be a lie.

"Meg, you're so cool," said Brad, our class president.

"Thanks," I murmured.

"Yes," agreed Janie, winking at me. "She sure is."

As the crowd broke up, I caught a glimpse of

Morris down the hall, writing in his notebook. He looked up for a moment and saw me staring at him. His eyes bugged out more than usual, and he ran off down the hall.

I smiled to myself. With my magic, I could finally have a chance to be smarter than my creepy brother.

# Chapter
# 6

"Megan. Megan Schuster!" Mom called from downstairs.

Oops. I knew that tone of voice. And whenever Mom called me by my full name, I was in trouble.

I dried my face with the towel and raced downstairs.

Mom was in the kitchen. She stood with her hands on her hips. "You've been neglecting your chores, young lady."

It was true. I was having so much fun with the magic, I even had trouble remembering to go to school in the mornings.

Jack's loud whine broke my thoughts. I looked down at our dog. He paced in front of the back door.

"You forgot to feed Jack. His food dish is empty."

"Sorry," I said to both Mom and Jack. I patted his black head and closed my eyes. A moment later, his dish was filled.

"I'm starving," I said as I reached for the milk in the refrigerator.

Morris was sitting at the kitchen table reading his science notes.

"After work I have to pick up my suit at the laundry and take Morris in for his eye exam," Mom said. As my mother filled me in on her day, I realized the milk carton was almost empty. She eyed the carton in my hand and sighed. "Are we out of milk?"

I knew I could help her out a little. I closed my eyes and wished. The carton in my hand became heavy.

"No, we've got plenty," I replied, pouring milk into my glass and over my cereal.

Morris looked up from his notebook to stare at me.

Mom glanced at her watch. "Kids, look at the time."

I glanced at the clock just as the school bus passed by the kitchen window.

I blinked my eyes closed and wished. When I looked again, the bus backed up, as though I were watching a movie being rewound.

I grabbed my books. "The bus is here. Bye, Mom. Love ya."

Morris was right behind me.

After I found a seat, I saw Morris staring at me. Did he see me use my magic?

# Chapter 7

I surveyed my overnight bag. Hmmm. Comic books, chocolate chip cookies, movie magazines, what else would I need? As an afterthought, I threw in a pair of pajamas and my toothbrush.

Madeline's slumber parties were the best. At the last one, her parents took us to Adventure Land and we rode the roller coaster seven times. We had pizza for dinner and stayed up talking all night. No one yelled at us even once.

Tonight we were supposed to go swimming in her built-in pool, so I packed my suit and towel. Zipping up the suitcase, I grabbed my purse and walked toward my closed bedroom door. I wished it open and walked through. Then I wished the door to close automatically behind me.

Once downstairs, I waited in the kitchen until I heard Janie's car honk for me.

"Good-bye, Mom," I said, giving her a kiss as she came in the front door.

She set her briefcase on the hall table. "Have a good time, Meg."

"See you tomorrow morning," I said.

"Do you want me to pick you up from Madeline's?" Mom called.

I turned around. "No, thanks. Janie's dad said he'd bring me home." I kissed her again. "See ya," I called, running to meet Janie and her father, Mr. Vanhooven.

"Have fun," Mom said, as she stood at the front door, waving.

I rolled down the car window. "Thanks a lot for giving me a ride," I said to Janie's father.

"No problem," he replied, pulling away from the curb. He glanced down at his gas gauge. The needle pointed to E. "But we'll have to stop for gas before we go to Madeline's."

Janie looked at her wristwatch. "Then we'll be late."

Mr. Vanhooven grinned. "Would you like to get out and push?"

I closed my eyes for a second. When I opened them, the needle had climbed to F.

"Look, Dad." Janie pointed to the dashboard.

Her father's eyes widened. "What in Sam Hill . . ."

"Maybe the gauge was stuck," I said.

He pulled into a gas station. An attendant came to the window.

"Fill 'er up, sir?"

"Yes, please," said Janie's father.

Janie and I turned to watch the mechanic. After he inserted the nozzle and gas splashed out, he said a few words I'm not allowed to repeat.

Mr. Vanhooven stuck his head out of the window. "What's the matter?"

"Mister," said the annoyed mechanic, placing the nozzle back on the gas pump. "Your tank is already full."

I sniffed. The smell of gas filled the car. As the attendant walked away, we saw his gas-stained trousers and soaked tennis shoes.

Janie wrinkled her nose. "Piiieeeeuuueee!"

Mr. Vanhooven stared at the gas gauge, shaking his head. "I guess you were right, Meg. The gauge was stuck."

Janie frowned at me and folded her arms in front of herself. Was Janie mad at me?

# Chapter 8

I sprinkled chocolate chips on top of my dish of strawberry ice cream.

"Sorry, Janie," I whispered. "I was just trying to help."

"Yeah, well, you made a mess." She picked up a spoon and walked away.

I couldn't figure out why she was upset. I had only tried to help.

"Making our own sundaes is a great idea," I said to Madeline, my wet hair dripping onto the towel over my shoulders.

She shook her head up and down in agreement and popped a maraschino cherry

• 49 •

into her mouth.

I helped myself to banana slices and nuts before I left the buffet and joined everyone around the pool.

Greta swirled her spoon into the hot fudge and caramel topping. "Fun party, huh, Meg?"

"You bet," I said. Scraping the bowl, I licked the spoon clean.

"Hey, Meg," called Susan from across the pool. "You're a great swimmer."

"Thanks," I said, smiling. I had won all three races earlier. I've always been good at swimming.

Janie frowned and muttered, "I wonder why you won."

I lowered my voice. "What do you mean by that?"

She looked up at me and mimicked Susan. "You're a great swimmer." And then she laughed. "Sure. With a little extra help."

My mouth dropped open. "I won those races without any . . ." I whispered, "Magic."

"Right," she said sarcastically, making circles in her ice cream with her spoon.

"Why, Janie Vanhooven," I said. "I wouldn't cheat."

"And how did your division homework get finished yesterday?" she asked.

I blushed, remembering. "Well, I did yours too!"

"Don't get mad." Janie finished her ice cream and dropped her spoon into the dish with a clatter.

Mad? Me? She was the one . . .

My angry thoughts were interrupted with Madeline's announcement. "Come on everybody. Let's play 'Hide and Seek'!"

"Yeah!" Cheers echoed around the pool, as we put our bowls away.

"Who wants to be 'It'?" asked Madeline.

"Janie does!" I yelled. I knew she hated being "It."

Janie's head jerked up.

"All right!" screamed Greta, her damp, brown hair sticking to the sides of her face. "Cover your eyes, Janie, and we'll all hide."

Janie obeyed and counted slowly. "One . . . Two . . . Three . . ."

Madeline hid behind the trash can. Greta climbed up into the oak tree, and Susan hid under the porch. And me . . . I closed my eyes and wished.

# Chapter
# 9

"Ten," said Janie, uncovering her eyes. "Ready or not, here I come."

I felt weird. I looked down to where my hands had been. Nothing was there. I stamped my foot. I felt the ground and heard the stamp, but I couldn't see my feet.

"I found Greta," cried Janie, pointing up to the branches of the oak tree.

Greta climbed down, while Janie searched in bushes, behind plants, and under towels.

"Ah-ah-choo!" The sneeze came from the porch. Janie ran to investigate and pulled out Susan. Next, she found Madeline behind the trash can.

"So where's Meg?" asked Greta.

Susan shrugged. "The last time I saw her, she was standing by the pool."

Janie folded her arms across her chest. "I've got a feeling we'll never be able to find her."

"Oh, come on," said Madeline. "You're giving up before you try."

"Right," said Susan scanning the backyard.

Janie sighed. "Oh, all right."

I sat down on a lounge chair. The metal scraped against the cement.

The girls whirled around and stared in my direction.

"What was that?" asked Susan.

Greta shaded her eyes from the evening sun. "I don't see anything."

"I'm not surprised," muttered Janie, walking slowly toward my chair. Not seeing my outstretched legs, she tripped over them, and tumbled right into the pool.

Quickly, I drew my legs under the chair as Susan, Madeline, and Greta ran to her.

Up came Janie, sputtering and coughing. Her long wet hair was draped across her face.

Madeline knelt by the pool's edge. "Are you okay?"

"What happened?" asked Susan.

Janie swam to the pool stairs and climbed out.

Greta handed her a towel. "Gee, it's a good thing you stayed in your suit."

I stifled a giggle. It really was funny.

Janie grunted in the towel as water dripped onto the cement. Madeline smiled. Soon all three girls bent over with laughter.

"It's too bad," Madeline hiccuped, "that Meg can't see this."

"I'm sure she can," said Janie angrily, drying herself off.

"Where is she anyway?" asked Greta.

Susan looked around the backyard. "It's like she disappeared into thin air."

"She did!" said Janie, throwing the towel to the ground.

"What?" asked Madeline.

Janie walked over to me and pointed to my chair. "Meg is right there."

I frowned. I should have known Janie would never be able to keep a secret. Especially when she was mad.

"Why do you think that Meg is in that chair?" asked Greta.

"Because I tripped over her feet."

"Janie," said Susan, putting an arm around her shoulders. "I think you've had too much sun."

"You don't believe me, do you?" Janie asked. She sucked in her breath and let it out slowly. "Well, I can prove to you that Meg is right here—invisible."

I panicked.

Greta and Madeline joined Susan and Janie around my chair. They had me surrounded. I stood up, careful not to make the chair move.

Since Janie had tripped over my feet, I knew they would be able to touch me. I wasn't like the ghosts in cartoons. What could I do? I had to think of something fast.

Janie put out her hand and squeezed my arm. She dropped her hand and gestured to me.

"Go ahead," she said to everyone. "Touch her."

# Chapter
# 10

I closed my eyes and wished. When I opened them, I found myself suspended in air, floating above them all. I looked down to see my four friends, huddled around the lounge chair, hands in the air.

"This is ridiculous," said Madeline.

"Come on, Janie." Susan grinned. "Where is Meg?"

Janie pursed her lips together. "She could be anywhere." Janie raised her voice. "Maybe we should tell your mother, Madeline. If she doesn't turn up, we'll have to CALL THE PO-LICE."

I shivered. The air was getting cooler since

the sun had set.

"Mrs. Slater!" called Janie.

Thanks a lot, Janie, I thought to myself. Looking around, I decided to hide behind the tree. I wished myself visible just as Mrs. Slater came outdoors.

"Well, girls, it's getting late. Why don't you come in and change into your p.j.'s. You can make popcorn and play in the rec room."

"But Mom . . ." Madeline began.

"We can't find Meg," interrupted Greta.

"What do you mean, you can't find her?" asked Mrs. Slater.

"We were playing hide–and–seek," Janie explained. "And she just disappeared."

I stepped out from behind the tree.

Mrs. Slater laughed. "Maybe you girls should get your eyes checked."

They followed Mrs. Slater's gaze. Madeline gasped. Susan's and Greta's mouths gaped open.

"Hmph," said Janie, folding her arms across her chest.

"I'll go in and start the popcorn," said Madeline's mother as she walked into the house.

"Where were you?" demanded Susan.

Greta put a hand through her short curls. "We were getting worried."

"Were you behind that tree all the time?" asked Madeline.

"I think she moved around a bit," suggested Janie, her eyes narrowing.

"Right," I agreed. "Why don't we go in now?" I moved toward the house.

I heard Madeline whisper to Greta. "I still don't know how she did it."

"I do," said Janie, slamming the screen door in my face.

* * *

That night, in our sleeping bags, Janie whispered, "Meg—Meg, are you awake?"

At first I pretended to be asleep, but then I changed my mind. It was hard to be mad at Janie for too long. And besides, she was the only one I could confide in.

I sat up and leaned on my elbow. "Is everyone asleep?"

"I think so." Janie played with the zipper on her sleeping bag. "I'm sorry about this afternoon."

I smiled in the darkness. She wanted to be friends again.

"Me, too," I said.

"Hey—do you want to go skating tomorrow night?"

"Sure," I said. "I'll ask my mom."

"Night, Meg."

"Night, Janie."

Maybe this time, I'd let Janie be a fancy skater, too.

# Chapter
# 11

Mom was in the kitchen when I got home. She was standing at the sink pouring milk down the drain. She looked up to meet my eyes. The milk kept flowing. We stood there for several minutes, watching the never-ending stream.

"You shouldn't waste it," I said, setting my sleeping bag onto a chair.

"Meg, what is going on around here?" she asked. She set the carton on the counter and whirled around to face me.

I broke down right away and confessed everything. I told her about how I suddenly found myself doing Janie's homework as well as my own. I told her how my magic refilled Jack's food dish, along with the milk carton and the peanut butter jar. And I admitted I got caught being invisible, but then wished myself up in the air.

I sank into a kitchen chair, exhausted. All this magic was wearing me out. Sometimes, I thought, I wished it would all go away. I looked at Mom. She looked tired, too—as though all of this news was too much for her.

Morris ran in through the front door, notebook in hand. He pushed his glasses up onto the bridge of his nose and squinted his eyes into slits, staring at me.

"How was your slumber party?" he asked, flopping into the chair next to mine. "Anything exciting happen?" He threw his notebook onto the table.

Mom cleared her throat. "Meg was telling me about . . ." She paused, giving me a chance to talk.

"Her magic?" asked Morris.

I stared at Morris in shock. "How did you know?" I asked.

"How did I know?" He shoved the notebook

toward me. "Read this."

My eyes skimmed the pages. Morris may be smart, but he sure is a messy writer. All I could read was, "Meg *scribble scribble* magic *scribble* wish *scribble*."

"I don't understand," I said.

"I made the magic." He smiled proudly.

"YOU?" I shouted. Then it was my turn to squint my eyes. "How?"

"I'm not exactly sure," he said. "That's the problem. I made a potion in my laboratory and sprinkled it on your doughnut."

I thought back to the day my magic had begun. "So that's why the doughnut tasted better than usual."

"That must be why you ate the whole box later," said Morris.

"The whole box?" I said. I had only eaten one, and then they had disappeared.

"But I lost the formula," Morris continued.

"I've told you time and time again to keep your room organized," said my mother.

"Will I have the magic forever?" I asked.

"I don't know. I've been studying you and taking notes to try to figure out how it works." He

doodled on the edge of the notebook.

"So that's why you've been lurking around, following me everywhere I go." Morris really made me angry. "You big snoop. I don't have any privacy anymore. I'm not your guinea pig!" I folded my arms in front of my chest. "Why don't you just take the magic yourself!"

"Sure," said Morris. "Wish it to me."

"Fine," I said. "I'm sick of it!"

# Chapter 12

I closed my eyes and wished Morris had the magic. I opened them. Morris frowned and looked at me intently.

"Make a wish," I said.

Morris closed his eyes tight. After a moment, he opened them.

"Well?" asked Mom, leaning toward him anxiously.

He looked at the table. "I wished for a laser printer," he said.

We looked around the room. Nothing had changed.

"I know!" he cried. He started to run up the

stairs, two at a time. "It should be in my room."

We followed Morris. We found him sitting on his bed, staring sadly at his old printer. We walked into the room, trying to walk around the piles of papers and test tubes and other junk.

"I don't understand," he said, shaking his head back and forth.

"Maybe I can't give the magic away," I said. "I know. I'll make your wish."

I closed my eyes and wished for the printer for my brother. I opened them. There, where the old printer stood . . . was the old printer!

"I don't get it!" I frowned. "Up until now, I've gotten every wish I ever asked for."

Morris took a stethoscope out of his desk drawer. "Stand still," he ordered. He listened to my heart.

"Hmm," he said.

"Anything wrong?" asked Mom.

"No," answered Morris. Next he took out his magnifying glass. He squinted through it, studying my face.

"What ARE you doing?" I asked, annoyed that I was the subject of his scientific research.

"You know, Meg. You don't need that magic.

Remember, you admitted the magic was getting to be a pain," he said.

"Yes," I said. "I even wished I didn't have it."

Morris and Mom turned to stare at me.

"Ohmygosh," I muttered quickly. "I wished the magic away!"

We sat in silence for a while, with only the ticking of the clock as background noise. The grandfather clock downstairs bonged five times.

"Well," said my mother. "I guess we should try to get things back to normal. Morris, it's your turn to set the table. Meg, don't forget to feed Jack," she continued. "He got into the garbage again, so he must be hungry."

"I don't need to," I said, thinking of the dog dish that was always full of food. "Oh, wait—you're right. Now that my magic is gone, so is the food."

We went downstairs to do our chores. I walked outside to fill Jack's dish. Then I stopped and stared. Looking around the backyard, I gasped. Dog food, bones, and toys littered the yard. On the deck, mounds of plain spaghetti, Jack's favorite food, were piled higher than Jack. He was busy wolfing it down.

"What in the world?" I said. "MOM . . . MORRIS!" I yelled. "Come out here!"

Mom and Morris rushed to the door. For a moment, no one said anything.

"Well?" I said to Morris. "You're the genius. What do we do now?"

Morris sighed and pushed his glasses up on his nose. "Guess I'd better get back to my laboratory."

## About the Author

Elizabeth Koehler-Pentacoff lives in California with her husband, their son, and a Yorkshire terrier whose favorite food is plain spaghetti.

Elizabeth is also the author of *Louise the One and Only*. In her spare time she likes to read, watch old movies, and go to the beach.

If *she* had wish magic, she'd wish for a refillable plate of chewy, chocolate double fudge brownies.